SPARKY & SPIKE

CHARLES SCHULZ and the
Wildest, Smartest Dog Ever

by BARBARA LOWELL

illustrated by DAN ANDREASEN

Sparky's dog, Spike, is a white dog with black spots.
He's the wildest and smartest dog ever.

Spike rings the doorbell to come inside. He only drinks from the bathroom faucet.

And he knows more than fifty words.

When Sparky tells Spike to fetch a potato,
Spike fetches a potato.

The most amazing thing about Spike is what he has eaten without getting sick—

Spike can even tell time.

Every Saturday night at 9 o'clock, Spike puts his paw on Sparky's dad's chair—it's time to drive down to the drugstore and pick up the Sunday comics. Spike is always right. He loves to ride in the car.

Sparky loves the comics.

His dad loves them, too. They read them together. Even Sparky's nickname comes from the popular comic strip character, Spark Plug.

(Sparky's real name is Charles, but only his teachers call him that.)

At school, Sparky's teacher passes out crayons and big pieces of paper.

Sparky draws a man shoveling snow. Then, he adds a palm tree.

"Someday, Charles, you're going to be an artist," Sparky's teacher says.

Sparky hopes it is true, but, he is not going to be just any artist—
he is going to be a cartoonist.

Only, drawing cartoons is hard.

Especially drawing the characters just right.

And school is tough. All the kids in his class insist that he draw on their notebooks.

But they only like his pictures.

When a comic strip exhibit opens at the library,
Sparky studies the original drawings closely.
He worries his drawings aren't good enough.

GOOD GRIEF.

Sparky rips them all up.
And he starts again.

Lucky for Sparky, he has Spike.

Spike gives Sparky a wild and smart idea. . . .

The comic strip *Ripley's Believe It or Not!*
is all about unusual people, animals, and things.

Spike is certainly unusual.
Surely Mr. Ripley will want to hear all about Spike.

Sparky draws Spike's picture on a letter to Mr. Ripley about the wildest and smartest dog ever.

Then he sends it off and waits.

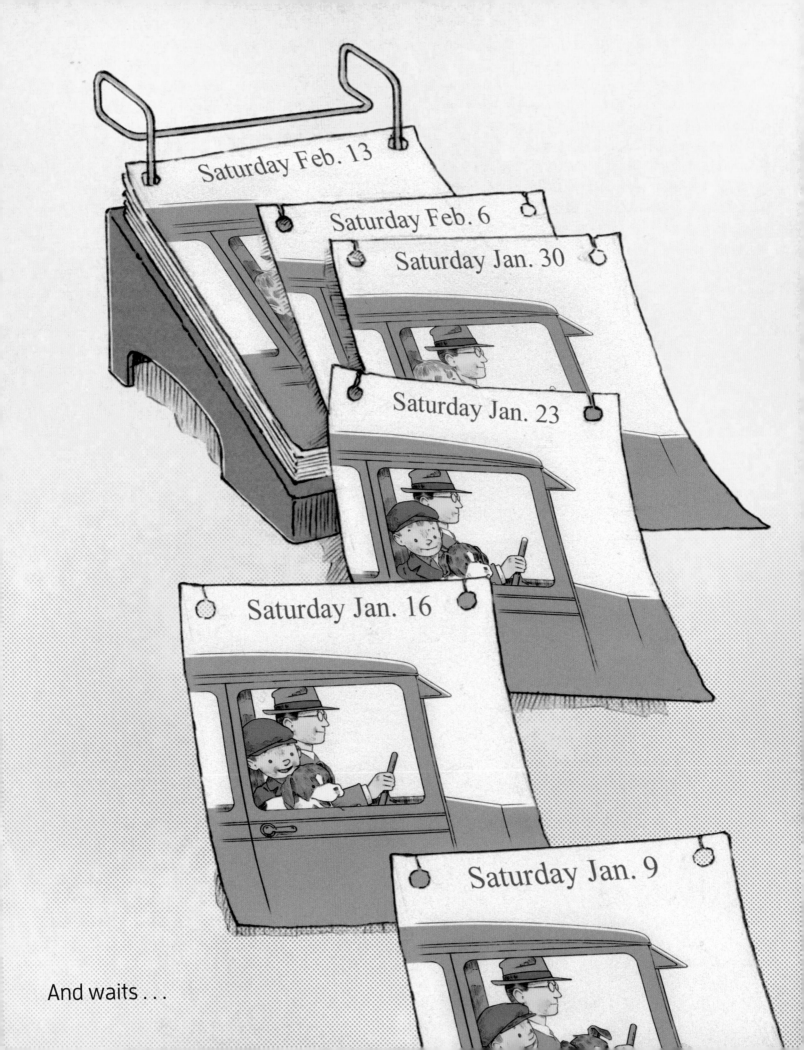

And waits . . .

And waits.

Every Saturday night at 9 o'clock, for two whole months, Spike signals to Sparky and his dad that it's time to drive down to the drugstore and pick up the Sunday comics.

And every Saturday night for two whole months, Sparky's picture of Spike is NOT in *Ripley's Believe It or Not!*

SIGH.

That's the way it goes.

Then it happens.

WHEW!

Believe it or not, Sparky's drawing is in the Sunday comics!
It won't be his last.

← Drawn by "SPARKY"

A HUNTING DOG THAT EATS PINS, TACKS, SCREWS AND RAZOR BLADES IS OWNED BY C.F. SCHULZ, St. Paul, Minn.

Sparky's drawings *are* good enough.

Someday, he'll have his own comic strip.

One character will always be the star—a white dog with black spots.
The wildest and smartest dog ever.

His name will be Snoopy.

CHARLES M. SCHULZ
NUMBER ONE SNOOPY PLACE
SANTA ROSA, CALIF. 95401

July 7, 1975

Daniel Andreasen
6759 Walter Road
North Olmstead, Ohio 44070

Dear Daniel:

It is difficult really to give a person much advice or help
when he is still as comparatively young as you are. I hope
that you will be able to get some of your work published in
your high school newspaper or something similar within the
next few years.

In the meantime, don't be impatient with getting started.
Draw as much as you can and read as much as you can.

Best regards,

Charles M. Schulz

CMS/ed

ILLUSTRATOR'S NOTE

Charles Schulz is an early and enduring inspiration to me. Just as Sparky sent a small drawing to *Ripley's Believe It or Not!*, I also at the same age sent a small drawing to a man I admired and hoped would respond with advice. After many weeks, a letter and a packet full of printed information about the cartooning business arrived in the mail. I will always be grateful that Charles Schulz took time to encourage an aspiring young illustrator. I did in fact take his advice to heart and worked as the illustrator for my school newspaper. And now I have a rewarding career as an author and illustrator of many well-loved picture books.

AUTHOR'S NOTE

Charles Schulz was born on November 26, 1922. His friends and family called him Sparky. By six, Charles had decided that he wanted to become a cartoonist. He practiced drawing his favorite comic strip characters: Buck Rogers, Mickey Mouse, Popeye, and the Three Little Pigs. In high school, he moved on to drawing characters from the popular action-adventure strips of the day. When Charles's mother showed him a newspaper ad from a Minneapolis-based correspondence school that read, "Do you like to draw? Send in for our free talent test," Charles responded to the ad and made the decision to enroll; they offered classes in cartooning. Ironically, he received a C in Drawing Children!

Charles began drawing cartoons of children with big round heads and adult vocabularies—forerunners of the children in *Peanuts*, who first appeared in print in four individual cartoons under the banner *Li'l Folks* and ran on Sundays in the *St. Paul Pioneer Press*.

Peanuts launched on October 2, 1950, in seven newspapers. There were four characters in the earliest strips: Charlie Brown, Shermy, Patty, and Snoopy. Charles soon added Violet, Schroeder, and siblings Lucy and Linus. Charles continued to add characters over the years, but the most popular was always Snoopy, the white beagle with black spots, inspired by Charles's own dog, Spike. When Charles added Snoopy's brother to *Peanuts*, he named him Spike.

Charles said Spike was "the wildest and smartest dog" he'd ever encountered. His *Ripley's Believe It or Not!* drawing of Spike appeared on February 22, 1937. While it's true that Spike ate pins, tacks, screws, razor blades, and rubber balls—and survived—most dogs would not!

Charles Schulz wrote, drew, lettered, and inked the 17,897 daily and Sunday *Peanuts* comics that appeared in over 2,500 newspapers from 1950 to 2000. Charles won the Reuben Award twice for best cartoonist of 1955 and 1964, given by his fellow cartoonists. In 1978, Charles was named the International Cartoonist of the year.

The last strip of *Peanuts* appeared on Sunday, February 13, 2000. Next to a drawing of Snoopy was a letter written by Charles Schulz telling his fans of his retirement and thanking them for their support. Just the day before, Charles M. "Sparky" Schulz died at his beloved home in Santa Rosa, California, at age 77.

To learn more about Charles M. Schulz,
visit the Charles M. Schulz Museum and Research Center in Santa Rosa, California,
or online at: https://schulzmuseum.org.

FOR NOAH, ADAM, CALEB, AND EMMA—B.L.

FOR EMMETT, VIOLET, EVELYN, AND ARTHUR—D.A.

Text copyright © 2019 by Barbara Lowell
Illustrations copyright © 2019 by Dan Andreasen
"Drawn by Sparky" illustration copyright © 2019 Ripley Entertainment Inc.

Book design by Melissa Nelson Greenberg

Library of Congress Catologing-in-Publication Data available.
ISBN: 978-1-944903-58-9

Printed in China.

10 9 8 7 6 5 4 3 2 1

Cameron Kids is an imprint of Cameron + Company

Cameron + Company
Petaluma, California 94952
www.cameronbooks.com